THE CHRISTMAS QUIET BOOK

By Deborah Underwood

Illustrated by Renata Liwska

HOUGHTON MIFFLIN HARCOURT

Boston   New York

57440
Manu-
factured in
Malaysia
TWP 10 9 8 7 6 5
4 3 2 1

Library of Congress Cataloging-
in-Publication Data is on file.

ISBN: 978-0-547-55863-9 hardcover
ISBN: 978-1-328-74056-4 paperback

The illustrations are drawn with pencil and colored
digitally. The text is set in Clichee.

For Santa, Mrs. Claus, and Dad, with love —D.U.
For Lynn, Ralph, and family (even Spice) —R.L.

Christmas is a quiet time:

Mysterious bundles quiet

Searching for presents quiet

Getting caught quiet

Hoping for a snow day quiet

Bundled up quiet

Snow angel quiet

Knocking with mittens quiet

Cocoa quiet

Nutcracker quiet

Too tall tree quiet

Shattered ornament quiet

Star on top quiet

Lights on quiet

Blown fuse quiet

Gingerbread quiet

Gliding quiet

Someone's dad is a costume designer quiet

Forgotten line quiet

Helpful whisper quiet

Mistletoe quiet

Breathing clouds quiet

Luminaria quiet

Early Christmas gift quiet

Aunt Tillie's pickle and banana stuffing quiet

Reading by the fire quiet

Note to Santa quiet

Listening for sleigh bells quiet

Trying to stay awake quiet

Christmas morning quiet